Living in Paradise

DC COMICS
SECRET HERO SOCIETY

FIELD TRIP DISASTER

Written by **Derek Fridolfs** | Illustrations by **Dave Bardin**

SCHOLASTIC INC.

Thanks to Bob Gale, for making time travel fun!

— *Derek*

ALL RIGHTS RESERVED. PUBLISHED BY SCHOLASTIC INC., *PUBLISHERS SINCE 1920.* SCHOLASTIC AND
ASSOCIATED LOGOS ARE TRADEMARKS AND/OR REGISTERED TRADEMARKS OF SCHOLASTIC INC.

THE PUBLISHER DOES NOT HAVE ANY CONTROL OVER AND DOES NOT ASSUME ANY RESPONSIBILITY
FOR AUTHOR OR THIRD-PARTY WEBSITES OR THEIR CONTENT.

THIS BOOK IS A WORK OF FICTION. NAMES, CHARACTERS, PLACES, AND INCIDENTS ARE EITHER THE
PRODUCT OF THE AUTHOR'S IMAGINATION OR ARE USED FICTITIOUSLY, AND ANY RESEMBLANCE TO
ACTUAL PERSONS, LIVING OR DEAD, BUSINESS ESTABLISHMENTS, EVENTS, OR LOCALES IS ENTIRELY
COINCIDENTAL.

ISBN 978-1-338-27329-8 (TRADE)   ISBN 978-1-338-58959-7 (SSE)

10 9 8 7 6 5 4 3 2 1   19 20 21 22 23

PRINTED IN THE U.S.A.   110
FIRST PRINTING 2019

BOOK DESIGN BY CHEUNG TAI
ADDITIONAL ILLUSTRATIONS BY ARTFUL DOODLERS LTD.

Diana,

Congratulations! I'd like to welcome you as our new student orientation leader.

You'll be on the front lines for welcoming new students to our school. You'll be there to provide them help as they adjust to our academy, to answer any questions they have and show them around.

As a foreign exchange student, you're ideally placed to offer your own experience as one of our newer students, and I'm sure you'll find things in common with those you help.

Thank you for your service. And don't hesitate to contact me if you need anything.

Sincerely,

James W. Gordon

Principal, Justice Prep.

Welcome to Justice Prep!

Here are a few rules to become a great student at our academy:

- Be polite.

- Listen to others.

- Be responsible and prepared.

- Be respectful.

- Be truthful and honest.

- Do your best!

- And always be <u>peaceful</u>.

I'm here to answer all your questions.

And if there's anything I don't know, then we'll go find out together.

REPORT CARD

STUDENT: Etta Candy
LEVEL: Three
HOMEROOM: Gordon
SEMESTER: One

Subject	Grade
READING	A
WRITTEN COMMUNICATION	A
MATHEMATICS	B
SCIENCE/HEALTH	C
SOCIAL STUDIES	B
ART	A
MUSIC	B
PHYSICAL EDUCATION	B

FAVORITE CLASSES: Is lunch a class? I have a sweet tooth. But I also like to read and write.

ATTENDANCE: Great attendance. Never absent. Sometimes tardy.

EXTRA QUALIFICATIONS: I'm told I have unbridled enthusiasm, boldness, school spirit, and a happy attitude. Many have called me "chatty" or "plucky," which is a fun word to say. Many of my teachers report I exceeded their expectations but can be too energetic, as if that's a thing. I look forward to working with you!

JUSTICE PREP

NEW STUDENT ORIENTATION FORM

- Take a tour of the school campus, playgrounds, cafeteria, gym, music room, theater, computer labs, and library.

- Explain classroom routines.

- Explain the school dress code.

- Assign lockers.

- Take the students to meet the principal and office staff.

LIST OF NEW STUDENTS

Karen Starr
Ralph Dibny
Caroline Ferris
Imra Ardeen

DIANA'S JOURNAL

I'm so thankful to be our school's new orientation leader. I figured it would be a nice chance to establish a good relationship with all the new students, the teachers, and see the school in a new light.

The first day of orientation went well, I think. At first I was worried when Priscilla didn't show up, but they assigned me another assistant in the nick of time.

What can I say about Etta? She's got so much energy and enthusiasm, it almost can't be contained inside of her. I wonder if it's because of all the sugar she eats. But I kinda think that's just who she is. It is a breath of fresh air to have someone excited to hang out with. It's so much different than my other friends. I mean, Clark is nice. And Bruce . . . well, Bruce is Bruce.

Still, I wonder whatever happened with Priscilla. I mean, we never much got along. But I hoped this would be a chance to work together and change that. I hope to have that opportunity again.

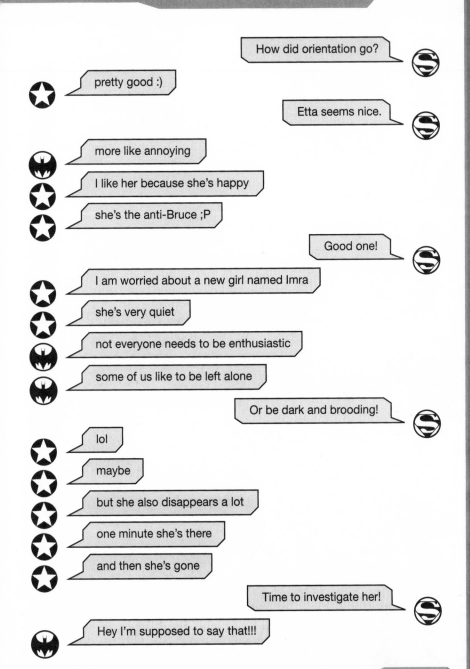

USERNAME: BWAYNE

INQUIRY = STUDENT SEARCH
LOCATION = JUSTICE PREP DATABASE
NAME = IMRA ARDEEN
ENTER COMMAND = LOCATE

PROCEEDING . . .

IMRA ARDEEN ----- RECORDS UNLISTED

CROSS-CHECK ALL DISTRICT DATABASES AND
PUBLIC RECORDS

PROCEEDING . . .

IMRA ARDEEN ----- UNKNOWN //
INSUFFICIENT DATA

RESULTS = INCONCLUSIVE

SEND

WRITE A MESSAGE

INTERVIEW RECORD SHEET
FIELD REPORTER — C. KENT

Question 1: Do you know who Imra Ardeen is?

"Whozzat?" — Harleen Quinzel

"I'm afraid not. But I'm fairly new to this school, too." — Arthur Curry

"Isn't she one of the newbies? Big deal." — Doris Zeul

"That's a funny name. Imra be right back with an answer. HAH!" — Joe Kerr

Question 2: Have you talked to Imra?

"Nope nopey nope." — Harleen Quinzel

"I haven't even seen her around, which makes no sense." — Mari McCabe

"She never talks to anyone. That's pretty cold." — Louise Lincoln

"No. Kind of a wallflower." — Pamela Isley

"It's the quiet ones you have to worry about." — Selina Kyle

Question 3: Is there anything you can tell me about Imra? (Where is she from? What school did she transfer from?)

"I think I saw her in the computer lab. Maybe she's a techie!" — Vic Stone

"Hands off, Clark. Don't horn in on my exclusive interview with her." — Lois Lane

"I hear she has a great disappearing act. We should exchange notes." — Zatanna

is everyone there?

not everyone hopefully

oh don't worry about Etta

she's harmless

what did you find out about Imra?

she doesn't exist

at least not on any school or computer database in any district EVER

and I checked them all

That doesn't make any sense. How is that possible?

she's hiding something and doesn't want to be found

like you in your cave! :)

ugh

I interviewed a lot of students. And no one seems to know her either.

I also checked about Priscilla

you did? where is she?

I borrowed some files from the school office

"borrowed"?

don't worry I put them back

after I got hi-res scans and uploaded them into my computer database

SEND

GROUP CHAT

 Priscilla has a long record of cutting class, being "sick," and other excuses

 Bad attendance is a delinquency offense. We should find her.

 and get justice

PEACEFULLY, Bruce!

while you handle that, I'll go find Imra

I know what class she's in

I'll go wait for it to let out and talk to her myself.

SEND

Where are we?

The future

Imra, how is your voice inside my head?

Telepathy

It's a power I have to communicate directly to you

Also you can call me Saturn Girl

It's what everyone calls me here

GET OUT OF MY HEAD!

It's entirely harmless

I'm not reading your mind, only sharing my thoughts with you

Your brain remains safe

NOT YOU, TOO!

heh heh

Let me take you to our base of operations

Our vid-terminal will be able to answer all your questions

22

IF YOU ARE READING THIS, YOU HAVE TIME TRAVELED INTO THE FUTURE.

WELCOME TO THE 31st CENTURY.

WE ARE THE LEGION OF SUPER-HEROES. A GROUP DEDICATED TO PROTECTING EARTH AND THE UNITED PLANETS.

ONLY THE BEST HEROES—THE BEST STUDENTS —WHO ARE WILLING TO HELP OTHERS MAY BE GRANTED MEMBERSHIP TO JOIN OUR RANKS AND BECOME A LEGIONNAIRE.

UNTIL THEN, WE HOPE YOU ENJOY YOUR VISIT.

AND PLEASE AVOID AFFECTING THE SPACE-TIMELINE CONTINUUM, WHICH COULD RESULT IN THE ULTIMATE DESTRUCTION OF OUR KNOWN UNIVERSE.

BE WELL.

LEGION OF SUPER-HEROES

LIGHTNING LAD / Garth Ranzz
Founding Member
Powers: Electricity, weather control
"Most Likely to Shock You"

SATURN GIRL / Imra Ardeen
Founding Member
Powers: Telepathy, mind control
"Most Likely to Read Your Mind"

COSMIC BOY / Rokk Krinn
Founding Member
Powers: Magnetism manipulation
"Best Personality"

PHANTOM GIRL / Tinya Wazzo
Powers: Intangibility (can phase through objects)
"Most Likely to Scare You"

BOUNCING BOY / Chuck Taine
Powers: Inflatable body, athletic bouncing
"Most Likely to Drink Your Soda Pop"

TIMBER WOLF / Brin Londo
Powers: Super-human strength, speed, and agility; sharp claws, enhanced senses, rapid healing
Voted "Best Hair" and "Most Likely to Howl at the Moon"

MEMBERSHIP YEARBOOK

CHAMELEON BOY / Reep Daggle
Powers: Shape-shifter
"Best Imitator"

INVISIBLE KID / Lyle Norg
Powers: Undetectable
"Most Likely to Disappear"

COLOSSAL BOY / Gim Allon
Powers: Grow and shrink body;
super-human strength and mass
"Biggest Smile"

STAR BOY / Thom Kallor
Powers: Ability to increase an
object's mass, density, or gravity
"Most Likely to Become a Star"

TRIPLICATE GIRL / Luornu Durgo
Powers: Ability to divide into three
identical bodies
"Triple Threat"

SHRINKING VIOLET / Salu Digby
Powers: Shrink to atomic size
"Tiniest Laugh"

TIME TRAVEL IS A FUNNY THING. I'M NOT SURE EXACTLY YOUR PART IN THIS. ONLY THAT YOU MIGHT BE ABLE TO HELP.

I JUST DIDN'T EXPECT STOWAWAYS.

HEY! THAT'S NOT OUR FAULT. YOU'RE THE ONE WHO—

YOU CAN COUNT ON ALL OF US TO HELP.

FIRST, YOU'LL NEED TO BLEND IN. YOU GUYS LOOK A LITTLE OUTDATED.

IS SHE CALLING US OLD?!

I PREFER RETRO.

WE'LL GET YOU DRESSED AND ENROLLED IN SCHOOL. THEN WE CAN FIND OUT WHO IS RESPONSIBLE FOR THE ATTACK ON THE SUMMIT.

NEW UNIFORMS? THAT'S GREAT!

THIS DOESN'T EVEN HAVE A CAPE OR EARS. I HATE THE FUTURE!

LEGION UNIFORM

Advanced polyfiber suit.
Nanite-linked under-texture provides
durable protection from harm and
temperature-controlled comfort.

LEGION BELT

Buckle communicator, homing
device; with warp-field
accessibility.

FLIGHT RING

Composed of the compound Valorium, with
antigravity capabilities, allowing the user to
fly at super-sonic speed. Willpower activated
with near unlimited potential. Flashlight
capabilities and can lift objects.

DATA-PAD

Thin, hi-tech, and
instantly portable. Who
needs a backpack or
computer to carry and
do your homework?

JUSTICE PREP

SO, YOU'VE TRAVELED TO THE 31st CENTURY

• BE AWARE OF YOUR SURROUNDINGS, WHETHER YOU WALK OR FLY.

• TECHNICALLY YOU DON'T EXIST HERE. YOU WON'T RUN INTO YOUR DOUBLE. SO DON'T MAKE A BIG DEAL ABOUT IT.

• AVOID CREATING A TIME PARADOX. WE'VE GOT ENOUGH TROUBLE IN THE FUTURE WITHOUT CLEANING UP YOUR MESS.

FINAL WARNING:

FINDING OUT TOO MUCH ABOUT YOUR OWN FUTURE CAN AFFECT YOUR PAST IN DANGEROUS WAYS. DON'T BE NOSY. LIVE YOUR LIFE BUT DON'T PEEK AT THE ENDING. NO SPOILERS.

LEGION OF SUPER-HEROES ENEMY DATABASE [THE FATAL FIVE]

EMERALD EMPRESS

Leader of the Fatal Five, Sarya uses a powerful mystical Emerald Eye of Ekron that floats and obeys her mental commands. It can shoot blasts of energy, allows her to fly, and grants super-strength.

THE PERSUADER

An outlaw who wields an atomic axe that can cut through anything. And he has enhanced strength and endurance as a result of living on a high-gravity planet. He was once recruited by the Legion of Super Heroes to help them, but later turned on them.

THAROK

A small-time crook who injured himself, vaporizing half of his body. He was rebuilt with robotic parts, increasing his intelligence and strength. And his robot mind allows him to control Validus.

MANO

A mutant born with an antimatter touch, allowing him to disintegrate anything he touches with his right hand. He once destroyed his home planet by touching it with the full power of his ability. He's forced to wear a special environmental suit to help him breathe.

VALIDUS

An enormous creature with super-human strength, strong enough to tear an entire planet apart with his bare hands. He can fire energy bolts from his brain. And is resistant to harm.

DATA-PAD JOURNAL ENTRY 01
DIANA PRINCE

THE FUTURE IS STRANGE AND INTERESTING, MUCH LIKE MY JOURNEY FROM PARADISE ISLAND TO SCHOOL. THERE ARE LOTS OF ODD AND NEW EXPERIENCES TO LOOK AT IN WONDER. ESPECIALLY THE ADVANCED TECHNOLOGY. I MEAN, THIS JOURNAL IS MY THOUGHTS THAT HAVE BEEN UPLINKED INTO THE DATA-PAD FROM A NEURAL CONNECTION TO MY BRAIN. I DON'T EVEN HAVE TO TYPE THEM OUT!

BUT WE DON'T HAVE TIME TO ENJOY THIS TRIP, BECAUSE WE HAVE TO STOP A DISASTER FROM HAPPENING. AND THEY THINK I'M PARTIALLY RESPONSIBLE FOR IT! I HAVE NO IDEA HOW THAT COULD BE, SINCE I'VE NEVER BEEN HERE BEFORE. I'VE BARELY EVEN TRAVELED ACROSS THE OCEAN TO GO TO SCHOOL.

THANKFULLY I'VE GOT MY FRIENDS CLARK AND BRUCE ALONG TO HELP OUT. IT WASN'T BY CHOICE, AND BRUCE ALREADY IS HATING HAVING TO ADAPT TO THE 31ST CENTURY. BUT I THINK THE THREE OF US, ALONG WITH THE LEGION OF SUPER HEROES, CAN STOP THE UPCOMING THREAT. AT LEAST, I HOPE SO.

SUPER HERO CLUB

Open auditions at the yellow rocket.
Prepare to face three challenges.
See Legion members for details.

Flying in circles?
Creating harmful smoke trails?
Get your jet pack fixed at **OTTO & AL'S REPAIRS**.
Student discount available!

NOVA EXPRESS TRAVEL

Trips to Mars and the solar system.
Book your summer vacation today!

ICE-CREAM EATING COMPETITION

Nine flavors from nine worlds.
Today in the cafetorium.
See Tenzil Kem to sign up!

FIELD TRIP TO THE INTERPLANETARY ZOO

See the new invisible eagle exhibit.
Deadline for permission slips
is this Wednesday.

HISTORY OF THE 21st CENTURY TO THE 31st CENTURY

PROFESSOR MICHAEL JON CARTER

The greatest hero you've never heard of…
teaching the greatest class you've never needed,
until now!

INSTRUCTIONAL GOALS

To provide you with my vast knowledge and time-traveling exploits throughout the centuries. You'll be wowed and amazed by my adventures, heroism, and grandiose personal insight into the man, the myth . . . ME!

At the end of this course, you will be able to learn the history of our universe, all the super hero buddies I call friends, and what it takes to be a hero.

Guest lecturers will include Rip Hunter and Blue Beetle (availability pending).

REQUIRED BACKGROUND

Download and read my authorized and unauthorized biography, *Gold Star: The Life and Times of Booster Gold*. And locate any further news-linked articles and vid-eps based on me.

REQUIRED MATERIALS

To successfully complete this course, you will need to bring the following materials to class: your data-pad, recording device (for photos and vid footage), and metallic autographing pens. Head shot photos provided for signatures (for a nominal fee).

Check out my sweet ride!

The Justice League needed my help to defeat Starro.

I saved the day again!

Meeting with my adoring fans.

I totally saved the president. I rock!

Fortune 500 welcomes me as their gold standard.

Premiere to my hit movie sequel.

My wall of fame.

42

PROFESSOR CARTER'S HISTORY ASSIGNMENT

1) What city was I born in?
   (hint: It has a lot of
   bats in it)

2) What sport did I play
   at the university?
   (hint: I was their star
   quarterback)

3) What's my robot's name?
   (hint: It's Skeets)

4) What's my hero name?
   (hint: It starts with
   Booster, and ends with
   Gold)

45

I'VE BEEN ALERTED THAT THE FATAL FIVE HAVE UPLOADED A COMPUTER VIRUS ONTO YOUR DATA-PADS. I'M CURRENTLY WORKING ON A PATCH TO STOP ANY DAMAGE, AND SHOULD HAVE IT FIXED SHORTLY. SORRY FOR THE TROUBLE.

– BRAINY

How is the timeline affected by me being here?

And how am I responsible for the accident at the peace summit?

All I know is something or someone from your 21st century is responsible

Maybe I'm responsible by traveling into the future

I don't think so

But you might be connected in some way

Whatever happens, we'll stop it

When is the summit?

Tomorrow

Need help with your homework, chores, or work?
Not super-powered enough to do it all yourself?
Get a CLONE today!

Want to learn martial arts?
Learn the tricks of SUPER KARATE!
After-school classes available.
See <u>Val Armorr</u> to sign up.

LOST AND FOUND
Missing arm lost on campus.
If found, please return to Floyd Belkin.
$ $ $ $ $ REWARD $ $ $ $ $

The Legion of Super Heroes doesn't want you—
but we do!
Join the LEGION OF SUBSTITUTE HEROES

Wanna get away from it all?
Manipulate time and space in the comfort of your
own alternate world?
Come view the latest in Pocket Universe
technology!
Contact the Time Trapper
(not available on weekends).

FLIGHT TRAINING with CAPTAIN HALL
"GET YOUR RINGS AND GET YOUR WINGS"

I come from a long line of aviators.
So it's my job to get you ready to fly safely.

We'll cover the following topics over the course of seven stages:

- **STAGE 1 =** The history of flight
- **STAGE 2 =** Introduction to flight rings
- **STAGE 3 =** Improving control
- **STAGE 4 =** Takeoffs and landings
- **STAGE 5 =** Air simulations
- **STAGE 6 =** Emergency landings
- **STAGE 7 =** Advanced piloting

All flight rings are composed of Valorium derived from Thanagarian Nth Metal, and possess antigravity capabilities. Further study in metallurgy is recommended.

For the purpose of my class, only the power of flight will be covered. To discover each ring's full capabilities of communication, projection, and matter manipulation, please consult the Legion of Super-Heroes.

52

FUTURE FINANCE
BUSINESS 101

Instructor: Dr. Alexia Luthor
Office Hours: By appointment

How to succeed at business and make a fortune in the 31st century

COURSE DESCRIPTION:

This course emphasizes the demonstration of business and finance strategies using the integration of current methodologies and practices, and skills learned and passed down by many generations of Luthors. By the end of our course, you will have the know-how to make as much money as you can and buy anything you want.

OBJECTIVES:

As a result of this course, you will be able to:

- Identify, locate, and navigate through the business industry

- Explain the theories to the success of LexCorp

- Collaborate effectively with your fellow students to create a framework for business growth and financial success

- Plan strategies to grow your market share

- Describe several effective tools for incorporating, wealth growth, and avoiding hostile takeovers

REQUIRED TEXTS:

- *The World According to Luthor*

- *Lexplinations: How to Become Rich and Powerful*

BUSINESS 101 – HOMEWORK ASSIGNMENT

All businesses require a development plan to establish a new venture as an entrepreneur. Every new venture should be required to come up with a detailed proposal plan. By coming up with a plan in advance, it helps to offset the costs and to budget. A good plan helps establish the vision needed to create a good business. With a plan in place, it helps management to think about the business, the objectives to its workers, and decisions to smooth the progress of planning.

First you need to break up into class groups of four. Decide who will be the boss of the company and who will be the workers. Decide what type of business you want to create and if there's a need for it. And then develop a plan for how to create it.

As a Luthor, my family controlled businesses in many markets, from property to industry to military and financial. Find something that you like, and create a business for it.

CLARK —

COME SEE ME
AFTER CLASS!

DR. ALEXIA

I'M SURE YOU'RE AWARE, THERE'S A LONG HISTORY BETWEEN THE LUTHORS AND YOU.

IT'S NOT ONE I'M PROUD OF.

I UNDERSTAND. BUT I'M LEARNING TO JUDGE THE INDIVIDUAL AND NOT THE FAMILY.

AS FAR AS I'M CONCERNED, YOU SEEM LIKE A GOOD TEACHER.

BUT IF YOU'RE NOT, THEN I'LL BE THE ONE TO SEND YOU TO DETENTION.

JUST ASK YOUR ANCESTOR, LEX.

INTRODUCTION TO DRIVER'S EDUCATION

Instructor: Space Cabbie

You're here because you failed flight training or you just want to learn how to drive a vehicle. And I'm here to teach you. It's up to me to help you identify the basic elements of becoming a successful driver, with the rules and regulations of the road and sky. I've got a lotta miles and experience as a laborer and pilot for hire. And a member of the "Cosmic Order of Space Cab Pilots" and "Veterans of Alien Wars." I also have my teaching credentials.

With that outta the way, here's our objectives:

1) To explain the structure of this here driving program and your responsibility for successful completion.

2) To list the basic driving fundamentals.

3) To identify the impact of decision-making on driving records.

4) To define the laws and restrictions of driving.

5) And to complete the course by obtaining a license.

Fill out and turn in your permission slip to be in this class. Once it's authorized, then go get your keys, meet me in the garage, and let's hit the road or airways. It's time to drive!

I MANAGED TO CREATE AN OFFICIAL PERMISSION SLIP FOR YOUR ENROLLMENT INTO THE CLASS. JUST TURN THIS IN AND YOU SHOULD BE OKAY. DELETE THIS MESSAGE!

– BRAINY

DRIVER'S EDUCATION
CERTIFICATE OF PERMISSION

Name: _____Bruce Wayne_____

Learner's Permit Number: _____19992001_____

School/Office Code: ____247247247_____

Parent or guardian's signature: _____

Teacher's signature: _____

MAYBE IT'S SAFER *FOR THE REST OF US* . . . IF SOMEONE JUST DRIVES YOU EVERYWHERE.

HMPFF! EVEN A THOUSAND YEARS IN THE FUTURE, I STILL NEED ALFRED.

AUTO SHOP CLASS

Taught by **THE MAIN MAN**, aka **LOBO**

Office Hours: No

(Special thanks to my friends at the intergalactic police work release program)

Looks like yer in trouble fer wrecking yer car, just like I'm in trouble fer blowing up a planet. As part of our punishment, we're stuck together. So I guess I'll train you how to fix an' upgrade yer vehicle, to get it in tip-top shape to hit the sky.

Hope ya brought some hooks, chains, laser saws, an' power drills. We'll hammer that metal hunka junk you call a car into place. An' once it's fixed, ya owe me a ride. I wanna go see the space dolphins, an' yer my ticket outta here!

DATA-PAD JOURNAL ENTRY 02
DIANA PRINCE

I'M STILL HAVING TROUBLE ADJUSTING TO THE FUTURE.

THERE ARE WEIRD CLASSES, WEIRDER TEACHERS, AND I'M STILL HAVING TROUBLE GRASPING ITS TECHNOLOGY (RINGS TO HELP YOU FLY, CARS TO HELP YOU FLY, AND CONSTANT DIGITAL ADS AND BULLIES).

WITH THE PEACE SUMMIT TOMORROW, WE STILL HAVE TO FIND A WAY TO STOP THE ATTACK. BUT WE DON'T EVEN KNOW WHO OR WHAT IS RESPONSIBLE FOR IT.

I ALWAYS HEARD THE FUTURE WOULD BE BRIGHTER AND MORE HOPEFUL. BUT I'M FINDING MYSELF JUST AS TROUBLED HERE AS I WAS BACK HOME. HOW AM I GOING TO BRING PEACE TO A WORLD I DON'T KNOW, WHEN I CAN'T EVEN BE PEACEFUL MYSELF?

I CAN HEAR MY MOTHER'S WORDS TELLING ME TO SET A GOOD EXAMPLE FOR OTHERS TO FOLLOW. TO BELIEVE IN MYSELF. AND TO TALK THINGS OUT TO FIND THE PEACEFUL SOLUTION.

MAYBE THE OLD WAYS STILL WORK EVEN IN THE FUTURE.

LUNCH MENU

All of our meals are prepared in our science labs with balanced protein, fiber, and vitamin supplements. Low in fat, low in sugar, and any allergens are removed and adjusted per student requirement. Eat with your friends in the cafetorium, or take it to go with a glass of high-energy natural water.

Today's selection includes:

TASTES LIKE CHICKEN

TASTES LIKE MYSTERY MEAT

TASTES LIKE SQUARE PIZZA

TASTES LIKE SALAD AND VEGETABLES

LUNCH SPECIAL

TASTES LIKE CORN DOG AND TATER TOTS

68

BOINNNG

100 DIGITAL DEMERITS EACH.

FLOAT WITH ME TO THE DETENTION ZONE.

THANKS FOR HELPING OUT! I'M BOUNCING BOY.

AND I'M DIANA.

71

THE RULES OF JOUNCE

The goal of the game is to be the last one standing who hasn't been hit by the ball.

There is no set number of players. The game is played in an enclosed cylindrical antigravity room. As the laser ball enters the room, each time it bounces off the wall, it picks up speed. If your body is hit, you're electrocuted and disqualified. If you catch the laser ball, you have the ability to throw it away or at another player.

There are three rounds. Each period, the ball will increase speed and number:

Round 1 = 1 ball
Round 2 = 2 balls
Round 3 = 3 balls

If there is no winner at the end of the third round, then it goes into overtime, where the ball will multiply with each bounce (causing multiple balls to be in play).

PLAYERS' STATS

(Scale of 1-10)

	AGILITY	SPEED	STRENGTH
DIANA PRINCE	8	8	8
SATURN GIRL	9	6	5
LIGHTNING LAD	6	8	6
PHANTOM GIRL	10	5	5
COSMIC BOY	7	5	7
BOUNCING BOY	3	2	10
TRIPLICATE GIRL	8	8	4
VALIDUS	6	6	11
THAROK	6	8	7
MANO	4	3	5

I can't believe I lost that game

It wasn't your fault

Someone cheated

Does it have anything to do with that EYE message?

It's possible

The Emerald Eye of Ekron is controlled by the Emerald Empress

She's the leader of the Fatal Five and always a problem

I'm only making things worse by being here in the future

I don't know what I'm doing, I'm a distraction, and I'm lost

Don't worry, being a new student isn't easy

But I'm here to help

That's what I'm supposed to be telling you as the orientation leader

Normally it's against the rules to show you too much

But I'd like you to see something

ATTENTION ALL LEGION OF SUPER-HEROES MEMBERS!

HIGH PRIORITY ALERT!

THE FATAL FIVE ARE ATTACKING THE LEGIONNAIRES' HEADQUARTERS!

DEFENSE SYSTEMS ARE ACTIVATED.

BUT ALL MEMBERS ARE NEEDED BACK AT BASE, IMMEDIATELY.

URGENT!!

ANOTHER ALERT?

From the Television Trouble-Finder!

ALEXIA LUTHOR!

I'm sorry for everything. But I hope you'll believe me when I say that it wasn't my intent. Really. Let me explain.

With enough money, you can buy anything. So I built a time machine using some of my fortune. I only wanted to use it to make even more money, in the future, or in the past . . . wherever.

But when I activated it, it transported someone through from the 21st century. They stole my time-travel device. And I've been trying to track them ever since.

93

TIME PERIOD: 21ST CENTURY

LOCATION: THEMYSCIRA – PARADISE ISLAND

PROBABILITY: IF THE CHEETAH CAN STOP DIANA FROM EVER LEAVING THE ISLAND, SHE WILL NEVER GO TO SCHOOL WITH HER.

I'VE HELPED PROGRAM AND HARDWIRE YOUR LEGION BELTS TO PIGGYBACK ON THE TIME STREAM COORDINATES FROM PRISCILLA'S TIME MACHINE. WHEREVER SHE GOES, YOU'LL BE ABLE TO FOLLOW. AND ONCE YOU FIND HER, YOU CAN STOP HER, AND ULTIMATELY DESTROY HER TIME MACHINE. ONCE YOU DO THAT, IT CAN RESET THINGS BACK TO NORMAL, AS LONG AS YOU FIND A WAY TO STOP PRISCILLA FROM EVER BEING TRANSPORTED INTO THE FUTURE IN THE FIRST PLACE.

BE CAREFUL TO AVOID YOURSELVES. YOU'LL BE TRAVELING BACK IN TIME WITH THE POSSIBILITY OF CROSSING PATHS WITH YOUR DUPLICATES IN THE PAST. AVOID ANY CONTACT AT ALL COSTS.

I WILL STILL BE ABLE TO COMMUNICATE WITH YOU FROM THE COMMUNICATORS IN YOUR LEGION BELTS IF YOU REQUIRE MY HELP. AND SATURN GIRL WILL TRAVEL WITH YOU TO MAKE SURE EVERYTHING WORKS OUT.

GOOD LUCK!

- BRAINY

IT FEELS LIKE WE BARELY GOT HERE. BUT WE HAVE NO TIME TO WASTE.

BEFORE YOU GO, WE HAVE ONE LAST THING TO SHOW YOU.

HONORARY LEGION MEMBERS

EVEN THOUGH YOU CAN'T STAY, YOU'RE STILL A PART OF OUR TEAM.

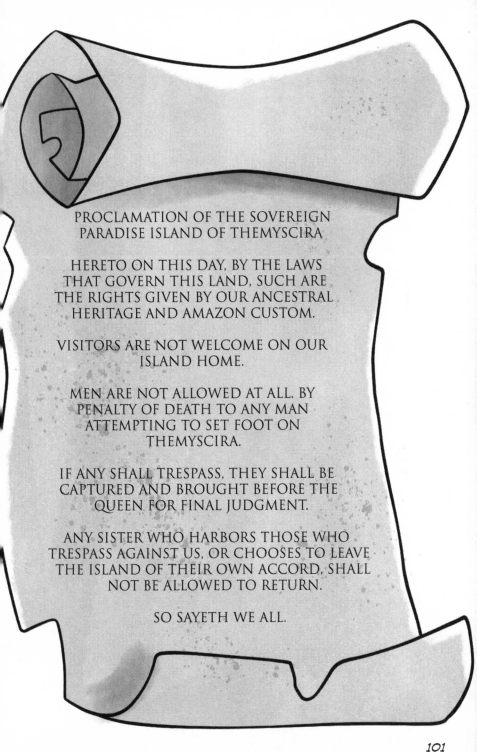

PROCLAMATION OF THE SOVEREIGN
PARADISE ISLAND OF THEMYSCIRA

HERETO ON THIS DAY, BY THE LAWS
THAT GOVERN THIS LAND, SUCH ARE
THE RIGHTS GIVEN BY OUR ANCESTRAL
HERITAGE AND AMAZON CUSTOM.

VISITORS ARE NOT WELCOME ON OUR
ISLAND HOME.

MEN ARE NOT ALLOWED AT ALL. BY
PENALTY OF DEATH TO ANY MAN
ATTEMPTING TO SET FOOT ON
THEMYSCIRA.

IF ANY SHALL TRESPASS, THEY SHALL BE
CAPTURED AND BROUGHT BEFORE THE
QUEEN FOR FINAL JUDGMENT.

ANY SISTER WHO HARBORS THOSE WHO
TRESPASS AGAINST US, OR CHOOSES TO LEAVE
THE ISLAND OF THEIR OWN ACCORD, SHALL
NOT BE ALLOWED TO RETURN.

SO SAYETH WE ALL.

THE AMAZONS OF THEMYSCIRA, AWAY FROM THE TEMPTATIONS OF MAN'S WORLD, STARTED A NEW LIFE ON THIS HIDDEN ISLAND. BLESSED BY THE OLYMPIAN GODDESSES OF ARTEMIS, ATHENA, DEMETER, HESTIA, AND APHRODITE, THE AMAZONS WERE GRANTED IMMORTALITY, GREAT PHYSICAL STRENGTH, BEAUTY, AND WISDOM. ARTISANS AND WARRIORS, THEY WISH TO LIVE A LIFE OF PEACE.

FOR CENTURIES, THE AMAZONS HAVE LIVED IN A PERFECT STATE OF HARMONY WITH THEIR SURROUNDINGS AND EACH OTHER, UNDER A THEOCRACY. THEY CELEBRATE THEIR CREATION EACH YEAR IN A FEAST OF FIVE, REMEMBERING THE GODDESSES WHO BROUGHT THEM TO LIFE.

EACH GENERATION, A CHAMPION AMBASSADOR IS CROWNED, TO LEAVE THE ISLAND AND BRING THE MERITS OF VIRTUE, LOVE, AND EQUALITY TO MAN'S WORLD.

AS DECREED BY THE QUEEN MOTHER HIPPOLYTA

A CONTEST
TO DETERMINE WHO IS THE MOST WORTHY OF ALL WOMEN

ATHLETIC ACTIVITIES SHALL INCLUDE ARCHERY, SPEAR THROWING, RUNNING, OBSTACLES, AND SWORD FIGHTING.

THE WINNER IS GRANTED THE RESPONSIBILITY OF JOURNEYING TO MAN'S WORLD, TO BE EDUCATED IN THEIR SCHOOLS, TO FIGHT FOR JUSTICE, AND BE AN AMBASSADOR FOR OUR PEOPLE.

DAUGHTERS ARE FORBIDDEN FROM ENTERING THE CONTEST
(THAT MEANS YOU, DIANA).

Remember, you must remain hidden during the competition

GAAAAHHHHH

A little warning next time you jump inside our heads!

No one must see you, so it doesn't upset the timeline from happening

We understand

Amazons wear armor and helmets to conceal their identities

I suggest you find some to stay hidden

Then get close enough to grab the time machine away from Priscilla if you get the chance

That's a good plan

Good luck

DIANA WINS ARCHERY

PRISCILLA WINS OBSTACLES

DIANA WINS SPEAR THROWING

PRISCILLA WINS RACE RUNNING

DATA-PAD JOURNAL ENTRY 03
DIANA PRINCE

I'VE NEVER BEEN MORE NERVOUS IN MY LIFE. AND I'VE BEEN HERE BEFORE.

THE FIRST TIME, I WAS COMPETING TO GET THE CHANCE TO LEAVE THE ISLAND AND GO TO SCHOOL. THIS TIME, I'M COMPETING IN ORDER TO STOP HISTORY BEING REWRITTEN . . . AND ERASING ME FROM IT.

THE OTHER DIFFERENCE IS I'M COMPETING AGAINST MY CLASS RIVAL. PRISCILLA AND I HAVE ALWAYS BEEN AT ODDS WITH EACH OTHER. SHE HATES ME ENOUGH TO TRY TO REWRITE MY LIFE. I DON'T KNOW HOW TO STOP SOMEONE LIKE THAT. TO CHANGE THEIR MIND ABOUT ME. TIME AND PATIENCE ARE LUXURIES I DON'T HAVE.

I JUST HOPE WHEN I COMPETE IN THE LAST EVENT TOMORROW, I CAN BEAT HER, EVEN IF SHE IS FASTER THAN ME. BECAUSE IF I DON'T, SHE MIGHT NOT STOP WITH JUST REWRITING MY HISTORY. NO ONE WILL BE ABLE TO STOP HER FROM REWRITING EVERYTHING.

AT LEAST BRUCE AND CLARK ARE HERE. THEY HAVE THEIR OWN SECRET PLAN TO GET BACK THE TIME MACHINE. WHATEVER IT IS, I HOPE IT WORKS — FOR ALL OF US.

STOP THE CHEETAH'S PLANS

1. DRESS UP LIKE AMAZONS

2. SNEAK AROUND PALACE GROUNDS

3. CLIMB TOWER WALLS

4. CRAWL INSIDE PRISCILLA'S ROOM

5. DESTROY TIME MACHINE

How are you, Diana?

Okay

The competition is tied

A winner will be decided in the final event tomorrow

I can barely sleep up here in the tower

Try to relax and remember you've done this before

I'm still in the safe house with the other Diana

We'll continue to hide here until you win and get back the time machine

Good night

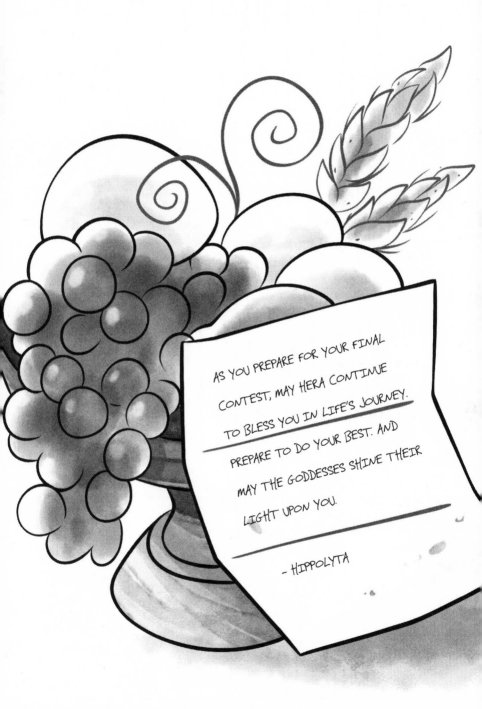

AS YOU PREPARE FOR YOUR FINAL CONTEST, MAY HERA CONTINUE TO BLESS YOU IN LIFE'S JOURNEY. PREPARE TO DO YOUR BEST. AND MAY THE GODDESSES SHINE THEIR LIGHT UPON YOU.

– HIPPOLYTA

CLUNK

WE HAVE A NEW CHAMPION!

AS YOUR VICTOR, I WISH TO TRAVEL TO THE OUTSIDE WORLD . . . TO GO TO SCHOOL.

DIANA?!?

SATURN GIRL, I'VE FOUND WHERE PRISCILLA HAS JUMPED IN TIME NEXT. I'VE UPLOADED THE COORDINATES INTO THE LOCATOR DEVICE, AND ADJUSTED YOUR BELTS TO MAKE THE JUMP.

MAKE SURE THAT YOU'VE WIPED THE MIND OF THE OTHER DIANA SO SHE DOESN'T REMEMBER ANYTHING BEFORE YOU LEAVE. THAT WAY HISTORY CAN REMAIN INTACT.

ONCE YOU LOCATE THE OTHERS ON THE BEACH, YOU CAN SAFELY MAKE THE JUMP. THIS TIME, YOU'RE GOING INTO THE FUTURE FROM WHERE YOU ARE. BUT NOT BACK HOME.

– BRAINY

DATA-PAD JOURNAL ENTRY 04
DIANA PRINCE

IT WAS INTERESTING TRAVELING BACK IN TIME TO THIS MOMENT. I HAD NO IDEA WHAT WAS IN MY FUTURE AFTER WINNING THE CONTEST THE FIRST TIME. BUT I'M THANKFUL I GOT TO WIN IT AGAIN, IF ONLY TO STOP PRISCILLA FROM REWRITING HISTORY. WE CAME SO CLOSE TO CAPTURING HER, BUT SHE MANAGED TO ESCAPE FOR THE MOMENT.

STILL, IT WAS FUN HAVING CLARK AND BRUCE ALONG TO SEE WHERE I GREW UP. MAYBE NEXT TIME THEY VISIT, THEY'LL GET A CHANCE TO ENJOY MORE OF THE ISLAND WITHOUT BEING ATTACKED. HEH HEH . . . PROBABLY NOT.

OUR NEXT TIME-TRAVEL JUMP TOOK US ALL BY SURPRISE . . .

This is your school, correct?

Yes and no

This is our original school, the evil one, before our current one

I'm not sure I understand

I guess not everything is in the history books about us

This is the school where we all first met

The principal and the students just happen to be evil.

That's it!

What?

Priscilla must be here to try to stop us from ever meeting

She was unable to stop me from coming to school

But maybe she could stop all of us from ever becoming friends

This makes things more complicated

Because now there's a much higher possibility that you can run into your duplicates here

What happens if we do?

It can destroy the space-time continuum and the universe as we know it

That only means one thing

We're going to need disguises

is everyone there?

Here!

yes

it's good to use our cell phones again in this timeline

and better this way

no more brain headache surprises

I never felt any of those.

that's because you don't have a brain

stop it! we don't have time for this!

Right

we need to stay split up in order to cover more ground

and find Priscilla

but not get seen

SEND

GROUP CHAT

from what we heard it sounds like they captured Clark and Bruce

Saturn Girl and I are going to try to locate where they're being held prisoner

you two need to help the other Diana

 Ducard Diana

ok I guess that's what we're calling her

help me

I mean help her from the bullying by Priscilla's gang of girls

and we'll report back later

SEND

SPLAT

I'll track their movements, and when no one is around, I'll spring a trap.

I can talk to them from above. They'll just hear my voice as a warning.

I've got traps set up all over school. We can monitor them back in the cave.

Using my super-speed, I can just tie their shoes together so they keep tripping. And they'll never see me do it.

I can interrogate them my way.

Or I can approach them my way.

anything new to report?

 Ducard Diana it still being bullied.

 There's not a lot of ways to help without being seen.

 I did find a way to disable the library Brainiac so it won't be a problem

I guess that's the one perk of being here again

knowing what threats to stop in advance

 I shut down the security cameras

 and Brainy was able to upload a virus to Brainiac to shut it down

just because we're successful with that

doesn't mean we're having any success dealing with the bullies

we've got to find a peaceful solution that doesn't involve getting seen

and find Priscilla before she changes even more of the timeline

SEND

The bullying here is getting out of hand. I can't go anywhere without someone trying to attack me and make my life miserable. And I haven't even done anything to them. Mother always said to find a peaceful solution, but it's getting harder to do that without anyone being receptive to it.

I think I'll try writing a note and leaving it in their lockers. But I'm struggling to find the right thing to say. Hera, give me strength!

NAME: BWAYNE
TO: CKENT, DPRINCE
SUBJECT: (FWD) DIANA JOURNAL

I WAS ABLE TO HACK INTO ~~DUCARD~~ DIANA'S EMAIL
ACCOUNT AND FOUND THIS JOURNAL ENTRY. TROUBLE IS
COMING. SO I THOUGHT YOU ALL SHOULD READ IT.

- BRUCE

< < < < < < < < < < < < < < < < < < < < < < < <
< <

RE: JOURNAL ENTRY

I TRIED THE PEACEFUL SOLUTION. TRIED TO WRITE
NOTES TO THE ONES BULLYING ME. BUT BEFORE I WAS
ABLE TO SEND THE NOTES OUT, THEY BROKE INTO MY
DORM ROOM AND DESTROYED IT.

I'M DONE WITH THE PEACEFUL APPROACH. NO MORE
DIPLOMATIC SOLUTIONS. BOYS AREN'T THE ONLY ONES
WHO SEEM BAD IN THIS WORLD. THE GIRLS CAN BE JUST
AS MEAN TO ONE ANOTHER, TOO.

I'VE BEEN TRYING TO HOLD MY TEMPER BUT I'VE HAD
ENOUGH. IF THEY WANT A FIGHT, I'LL GIVE IT TO
THEM. THEY HAVE NO IDEA WHO THEY'RE DEALING WITH!

SCHOOL NURSE INCIDENT REPORT

STUDENT: Harleen Quinzel, Circe, Doris Zeul, Louise Lincoln

TEACHER: unlisted

CLASS: unlisted

DATE: September 19

DESCRIPTION OF THE INCIDENT:

When I arrived at school today, many injured students were waiting in the hallway to see me: one with a fractured arm from being stuffed into a trash can, others with bumps and bruises. Some claim they were forced to tell the truth, but weren't sure how they were coerced. And others have stained clothes and matted hair from a cafeteria food fight.

ACTION TAKEN:

Most students were administered light first aid treatments of bandages or referred to the school guidance counselor to share their feelings.

FURTHER RECOMMENDED CARE:

None at this time. Although if this keeps up, you might want to hire additional staff to help in the school nurse office. I'm not a hospital or clinic, you know!

IF YOU HAVE ANY QUESTIONS ABOUT THIS EVENT, PLEASE CALL THE NURSE'S OFFICE.

DUCARD ACADEMY

TEACHER LEAVE REQUEST FORM

TEACHER NAME: Jervis Tetch

SUBJECT MATTER TAUGHT: English Literature

DATE(S) REQUESTED: Immediate

PLEASE EXPLAIN THE REASON FOR THE REQUEST:

I am unable to get my students to listen to me or do what I tell them. I need more time away to continue my development of new methods to control the minds of others. Or I will certainly go mad.

One student in particular stands out as trouble. Her name is Diana Prince. She continues to mock me, prank me, and rile the rest of the students against me. She is a belligerent ignoramus and not worthy of this learning institution. I suggest her removal from this class, removal from this school, or removal from this district. I hope that by bringing this to the attention of our school principal, he might find a spot better suited for her.

Dear Parents/Guardians of Diana Prince,

We would like to inform you of a growing situation with your child.

It has been brought to my attention that your child has become a problem at our school. There are multiple reports of your child disrupting classes, being uncivil on campus, getting into fights with teachers and students, and being absent.

In general, your child is disturbing our peaceful institution.

By bringing this to your attention, we wish to speak with you in conference and in person. Call our office to set up an appointment at your earliest convenience. If you have any further questions or concerns, please contact our main office.

Thank you for your support.

GROUP CHAT

how is my other self doing?

Superman: Uhh you don't want to know.

that bad?!

Superman: She's letting her temper control her.

Superman: She's almost as bad as the bullies she's beating up.

Batman: I kind of like this version of her

Batman: can we keep her?

shut up Bruce! :P

Superman: Without having Bruce and Clark as friends

Superman: or forming the Criminal Investigation Unit

Superman: she's just angry all the time

Batman: Cheetah found a way to erase the old Diana

Batman: and this new Diana is worse, I guess

SEND

GIRLS' PHYSICAL EDUCATION
COACH KITTY Class of Hard Knocks

NOTE TO PRINCIPAL = I thought you'd like to know how impressed I am with two students in my class, Diana Prince and Priscilla Rich. Both show exemplary athleticism, scoring high marks, while beating all the other students in my class. They are distancing themselves even from my previous best student, Talia, while breaking records and breaking their fellow classmates.

If you're looking to add students to your special program, I believe these two candidates are perfect for what you require.

STUDENT EVALUATION REPORT

STUDENT: <u>Diana Prince</u>   PROFESSOR: <u>Hugo Strange</u>

Which of the following best describes you?
Choose only one:

❏ Ambitious ☒ Angry ❏ Bored ❏ Calm ❏ Confused ❏ Creative ❏ Embarrassed
❏ Excited ❏ Focused ❏ Happy ❏ Hungry ❏ Lonely ❏ Loved ❏ Patient
❏ Proud ❏ Relieved ❏ Sad ❏ Scared ❏ Surprised ❏ Tired ❏ Other

Please rate the following based on how you are feeling about each area
of your life:

Friendships
Terrible   Great
1   2   3   4   5   6   (7)   8   9   10

Home/Family
Terrible   Great
1   2   (3)   4   5   6   7   8   9   10

Grades/School
Terrible   Great
1   2   3   (4)   5   6   7   8   9   10

Diagnosis:

As a foreign exchange student, Diana should struggle to fit in and
belong. But she's really tapped into her temper and anger and is getting
everything she wants. No one bullies her anymore. No one challenges her.
She has no true friends besides the other bullies that she's scared into
submission. Even the teachers are afraid of her. I feared she might be
too hard to break and too tough to handle. But she's proved me wrong.

Special Notes:

She's exactly who we want. A perfect candidate for the Nanda Parbat
program. It is time for her to meet the principal. Just don't hold it against
her that she's scoring higher than your daughter in athletics.

things have taken a turn

what's going on?

you know how Priscilla and you used to be enemies?

now you're fast friends

the other you I mean

how is this possible?

She's beaten up and scared all of her bullies and teachers.

They give her whatever she wants now out of fear.

fear is powerful

She's on the cheer squad. She's friends with Priscilla and her gang.

and she's on her way to meeting the principal and you know what that means

they want to train me to join their evil League of Shadows!

Any luck on your end?

Saturn Girl and I haven't been able to find where the prisoners are held

but we're searching as many classrooms as we can

SEND

TIRED OF WORKING ALONE
TO RULE THE WORLD?

SEEKING A GROUP TO
DO IT WITH?

LET'S GANG TOGETHER AND
COME UP WITH THE SOLUTION.

MEET IN THE LIBRARY AFTER SCHOOL
AND JOIN OUR "CHEETAH PACK"!

NO BOYS ALLOWED

The claws come out!

Boys ruin everything.
It's time for a girl to lead.

Lex tries to buy the election.

Money can't buy everything.

Say mrreow to your new
class president!

THE DUCARD DAILY

NOVEMBER 6

ELECTION RESULTS:
NEW CLASS PRESIDENT WINS
IN A RUNAWAY VICTORY!!!

LETTER FROM THE PRESIDENT by Priscilla Rich

You don't have to have money to win an election, but it doesn't hurt to be Rich . . . Priscilla Rich! Thank you for your vote. As your new class president, I'm going to hit the ground running. I ran this race as fast as I could, and now I want to do the same for this school. All of you are part of my "Cheetah Pack" now (girls, anyways). It's time for us to control this school and our future. And it's my promise that we'll get everything we want . . . everything I want. And I have all the time to do it. Thank you!

GROUP CHAT

161

FAREWELL, MY BELOVED DUCARD SCHOOL.

IT'S TIME FOR FATHER AND ME TO ESCAPE FROM THIS CRAZY PLACE!

YOU'RE NOT LEAVING BEFORE I GET ANSWERS.

I WANT THE TRUTH ABOUT WHY YOU'RE DOING ALL THIS, PRISCILLA!

DATA-PAD JOURNAL ENTRY 05
DIANA PRINCE

AFTER JUMPING ALL THROUGHOUT TIME, INTO THE FUTURE AND THE PAST, WE WERE FINALLY ABLE TO CATCH UP TO PRISCILLA. AND USING MY LASSO OF TRUTH, I WAS FINALLY ABLE TO GET AN HONEST ANSWER ABOUT WHY SHE WAS INVOLVED.

PRISCILLA HATES COMING IN SECOND EVERY TIME WE COMPETE. SHE HATES THAT I SCORE HIGHER ON TESTS, WIN MORE ATHLETIC EVENTS, HAVE MORE TRUE FRIENDS, AND THAT I'M THE ORIENTATION LEADER WHILE SHE'S ONLY MY ASSISTANT.

JEALOUSY IS THE REASON SHE HATES ME SO MUCH. AND I HAD NO IDEA UNTIL SHE TOLD ME.

I NEVER WANTED TO MAKE HER MY ENEMY. AND ANY COMPETITION WE'VE HAD, I ALWAYS CONSIDERED FUN AND INNOCENT. BUT IT'S MADE ME RETHINK HOW OTHERS FEEL. JUST BECAUSE I'M NOT CLOSE TO SOMEONE DOESN'T MEAN I CAN'T EMPATHIZE WITH THEM. I NEVER MEANT HER ANY HARM, AND I'M SORRY SHE TOOK IT THAT WAY.

TIRED OF LIVING IN MY SHADOW, SHE DITCHED ORIENTATION AND SCHOOL AS SOON AS THE TIME PORTAL OPENED UP, CLIMBING INSIDE, IT BROUGHT HER TO A FUTURE WITHOUT ME, BUT IN SOME WAYS, HISTORY STILL CAUGHT UP WITH HER. SHE TRIED TO DESTROY ANY PROOF OF MY EXISTENCE, BUT LUCKILY WE WERE ABLE TO STOP HER.

NOW THERE'S ONLY ONE THING LEFT TO DO. WE NEED TO COMPLETELY RESTORE THE TIMELINE, GO BACK TO THE MOMENT BEFORE PRISCILLA LEFT, AND STOP HER FROM GOING INTO THE FUTURE. IF WE DO THAT, WE CAN CLOSE THIS TIME LOOP AND STOP IT FROM EVER HAPPENING.

WHEN I ASKED HER WHERE THE TIME PORTAL OPENED, SHE SAID IT WAS NEAR THE GIRLS' LOCKER ROOM. SO MAYBE THERE'S STILL ENOUGH TIME TO MAKE THIS RIGHT.

PRIVATE TEXT MSG
*** FOR DIANA'S EYES ONLY ***

HELLO, DIANA. IF YOU'RE READING THIS, THEN YOU KNOW I'M THE ONLY ONE WHO HAS ACCESS TO YOUR ACCOUNT AND PASSWORD.

SO WHY AM I WRITING THIS TO MYSELF?

I HAVE A SPECIAL REQUEST TO ASK YOU . . . . TO ASK MYSELF.

CAN YOU LET PRISCILLA BE THE ORIENTATION LEADER?

I KNOW YOU VOLUNTEERED AND WERE AWARDED THAT POSITION BY THE PRINCIPAL. BUT NOW I'M ASKING YOU TO VOLUNTEER TO GIVE IT TO SOMEONE WHO WOULD CHERISH IT EVEN MORE THAN YOU.

SOMETIMES IT'S BETTER TO GIVE THAN TO GET. TO LOSE SOMETHING IN ORDER TO GAIN A PEACEFUL RESOLUTION. AND SHE COULD REALLY USE IT.

PLEASE CONSIDER IT. THANK YOU.

Normally I would have to adhere to time-travel protocol

To wipe the minds of everyone in order to preserve their future

But since you were successful in stopping Priscilla from going to the future this time

It erased that event from ever happening

There's no mind wipe necessary

Brainy will explain it all to you before you forget

Since this is the last time I talk to all of you, let me say it's been an honor getting to meet the heroes I've always looked up to

You didn't disappoint

See you in the future

NORMALLY WHEN THE TIMELINE IS RESTORED, EVERYONE WOULD BE ERASED IN THE PROCESS, AS IF IT NEVER HAPPENED. BUT I'VE BEEN ABLE TO DELAY THAT SLIGHTLY BY ACTIVATING A TIME DISPLACEMENT FIELD GENERATED BY YOUR BELTS.

YOU ALL HAVE A MOMENT TO BE OBSERVERS AND WATCH THE RESULT OF YOUR HEROIC ACHIEVEMENT WITHOUT BEING SEEN. AND THIS BRIEFEST OF MOMENTS FOR ME TO THANK YOU AS WELL.

YOU REALLY ARE HEROES!

ONCE YOU PRESS YOUR BELTS, IT WILL DEACTIVATE YOUR TIME DISPLACEMENT FIELDS, AND YOU'LL DISAPPEAR AS THE TIMELINE IS RESTORED.

THANKS FOR EVERYTHING!

- BRAINY

PRINCIPAL-STUDENT REQUEST FORM

Student: DIANA PRINCE

RE: ORIENTATION LEADER

Thank you for awarding me the position of student orientation leader. But upon further review, I'd like to make a request that Priscilla Rich be given that position instead.

I've noticed she's never been thought of for positions like this, and I'd like to change that. As a quick learner and just quick in general, she'd be great at running the new students around campus and assisting them. Even better . . . I know that she's interested!

I'd still be happy to help as her assistant. But I look forward to her taking on the role of the new student orientation leader.

Sincerely,

Diana

QUICK ANNOUNCEMENT. I AM NO LONGER YOUR ORIENTATION LEADER.

AND THAT'S OKAY. BECAUSE I KNOW SOMEONE WHO WILL DO IT EVEN BETTER.

SO LET ME INTRODUCE YOU TO PRISCILLA RICH, YOUR NEW STUDENT ORIENTATION LEADER.

WELL, THERE'S LOTS TO SEE, SO LET'S GET RUNNING!

MESSAGES

GROUP CHAT

How was student orientation?

Great!

but I was only the assistant

Priscilla was the leader

I thought you were the leader

I was

but I let her have it

and she did great

first you wanted it, volunteered for it, then gave it away

why do girls always change their minds?

it's because we have minds to change

and aren't as short-minded as the boys

Good one!

let's all get together for lunch

I have someone I want to introduce you to

she's my new friend Etta

you'll like her Bruce

I sure hope so

SEND

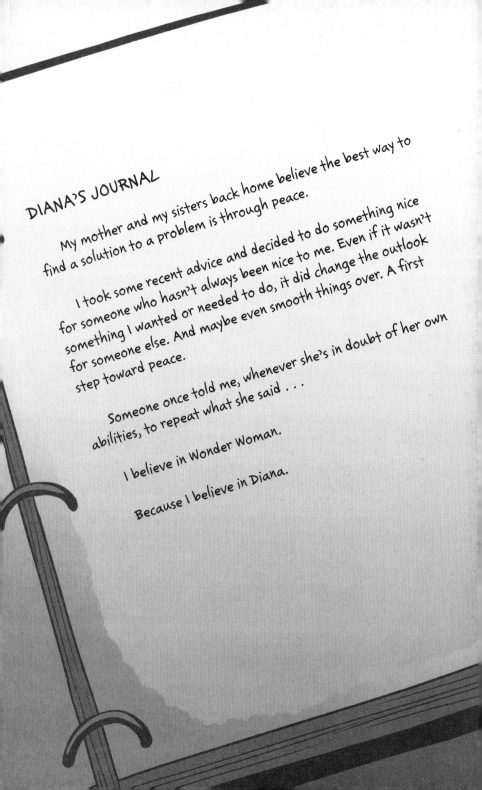

DIANA'S JOURNAL

My mother and my sisters back home believe the best way to find a solution to a problem is through peace.

I took some recent advice and decided to do something nice for someone who hasn't always been nice to me. Even if it wasn't something I wanted or needed to do, it did change the outlook for someone else. And maybe even smooth things over. A first step toward peace.

Someone once told me, whenever she's in doubt of her own abilities, to repeat what she said . . .

I believe in Wonder Woman.

Because I believe in Diana.

Hello, my daughter. I'm so happy to hear that you're doing well in school and as a great ambassador to the world. Study hard, be at peace, and keep up the great work!

Love, Mom

PS No matter how many times you ask, boys are never allowed to visit the island. EVER! They're nothing but trouble. X O X O

Derek Fridolfs

Derek Fridolfs is a *New York Times* bestselling writer. With Dustin Nguyen, he co-wrote the Eisner-nominated *Batman: Li'l Gotham*. He's also worked on a range of titles including *Arkham City* with Paul Dini, *Adventures of Superman*, *Detective Comics*, *Sensation Comics Featuring Wonder Woman*, and *Biff to the Future* with producer/screenwriter Bob Gale. He's written and drawn comics based on the cartoons for *Adventure Time*, *Regular Show*, *Clarence*, *Pig Goat Banana Cricket*, *Pink Panther's The Inspector*, *Dexter's Laboratory*, *Teenage Mutant Ninja Turtles*, *Teen Titans Go!*, *Looney Tunes*, and *Scooby-Doo, Where Are You!* He's also written chapter books for Capstone based on the Justice League.

Dave Bardin

Dave Bardin is an award-winning illustrator who has worked in comics, commercials, music videos, video games, magazines, television, and book publishing. He has illustrated over twenty children's books including titles for Bad Robot, Graphic India, Leap Frog, Little Brown, Scholastic, Pearson, ABDO, Cartoon Network, Marvel, and DC. He lives and works in Los Angeles.